To lovely Harris, thank you – SK
To Janine Louise Boursain – ST

SIMON AND SCHUSTER
First published in Great Britain in 2010 by Simon and Schuster UK Ltd
1st Floor, 222 Gray's Inn Road, London WC1X 8HB
A CBS Company
Text copyright © 2010 Sarah KilBride
Illustrations copyright © 2010 Sophie Tilley
Concept © 2009 Simon and Schuster UK
The right of Sarah KilBride and Sophie Tilley to be identified
as the author and illustrator of this work has been asserted by them
in accordance with the Copyright, Designs and Patents Act, 1988
All rights reserved, including the right of reproduction in whole or in part in any form
A CIP catalogue record for this book is available from the British Library upon request
ISBN: 978 1 4711 7462 9
Printed in China
1 3 5 7 9 10 8 6 4 2

Willow
the Magic Forest Pony

Princess Evie's Ponies

Willow the Magic Forest Pony

Sarah KilBride

Illustrated by Sophie Tilley

SIMON AND SCHUSTER

London New York Sydney

The sun was shining at Starlight Stables as Princess Evie led Willow out of her horsebox. Willow was still wearing the bright pink rosette they had won at the gymkhana.

"Well done, Willow!" said Evie. "First prize again.
Let's go on an adventure to celebrate."
Willow was a magic pony, just like all of Princess Evie's
other ponies. Whenever Evie rode her, she was whisked
away on a magical adventure in a faraway land.

Willow gave a whinny. She LOVED an adventure!

Evie threw on her rucksack full of useful things
and swung herself onto Willow's back.

Her kitten, Sparkles, miaowed and joined her.

With no time to lose, the friends were
cantering towards the tunnel of trees.
Evie looked back and saw the stables and
horsebox grow smaller and smaller in the distance.
Where would the tunnel take them today?

Suddenly, they were trotting through
the most magical forest. Princess Evie's hair was
decorated with pretty wild roses and she was wearing
a primrose yellow dress. Willow's mane and tail
shimmered with garlands of woodland flowers and leaves.

"Where are we?" whispered Evie, looking high into the branches.

Then she spotted a whole host of forest fairies.

"Hooray! You're here at last!" they called. "We've been waiting for you."

The fairies were preparing for the
Bluebell Forest Fashion Show and they needed
Princess Evie's help. They led her to a clearing
where everyone was busy at work.

Some fairies were using silver spiders' webs to sew delicate outfits, others were using sparkling dewdrops to decorate them. Evie helped to scatter cushions on the forest floor for the audience. Finally, after a great deal of fussing and fluttering, everything was ready.

The outfits were arranged neatly on rails, the
stage was decorated with flowers and the glow-worms
were ready to light up the show with their tails.
"I think it's time for a break!" said Holly, the tallest fairy.
"Come on, let's go to Acorn Café for a treat."

All the fairies skipped along happily and
settled themselves at the tables.

"Thank you for helping us, Evie," smiled Holly,
as she offered her a cup of elderflower sparkle
and some delicious wild strawberries.

After their snack, everyone made their way back
to the clearing to get ready for the show but –
oh no! – the clothes rails were completely empty!
Every single outfit had vanished!
Where could they have gone?

Princess Evie rummaged in her rucksack
and pulled out a magnifying glass.
"Look!" she cried. "Footprints!"

Evie and Sparkles jumped up onto Willow's back.
"Come on, Holly! There's room for one more!" said Evie.

They followed the footprints to a little green door.

"Hazel's house!" said Holly. "That's strange!

Why would Hazel take our outfits?"

The door swung open and there stood a very angry forest fairy.

"I took them," hissed Hazel, "because I wasn't invited

to the fashion show!"

"But I left your invitation here," said
Holly, pointing to a stone. "Where has it gone?"

Just then, Willow shook her mane.

"Well done, Willow!" said Evie, as she spotted some tiny footprints.

The friends followed the footprints . . .

. . . to Missy Mouse's house. Missy was busy spring cleaning
when, suddenly, Sparkles dived into her
beautiful nest and started to pull it apart.

"That's not very polite!" cried Evie, but then she noticed
the nest was made from wool, twigs and
shredded golden invitation!

"Well done, Sparkles!" said Evie.

"You've found the missing invitation!"

Hazel and Missy said sorry for their mistakes.

Then everyone gathered together the outfits and rushed

back to the clearing.

All the forest fairies cheered when they saw their glittering dresses and they quickly changed. Backstage was buzzing with excitement as the audience began to arrive and the music started to play.

"Wait! Wait!" cried Evie. "Someone has forgotten their outfit!"

Hanging alone on the rail was a dress of pink petals
and tiny dewdrops that sparkled like little diamonds.

"That's for you," smiled Holly.

The fairies had made it for Evie.

It was beautiful!

It was time for the show to begin! The glow-worms lit up the stage with their bright tails and a choir of birds sang their favourite forest songs. The audience sat on the velvety cushions and clapped as the forest fairies took it in turns to swirl down the catwalk.

Princess Evie, Hazel and Holly swayed down the catwalk together, their flowery outfits shimmering. Sparkles purred, Willow neighed and Missy Mouse squeaked with delight!

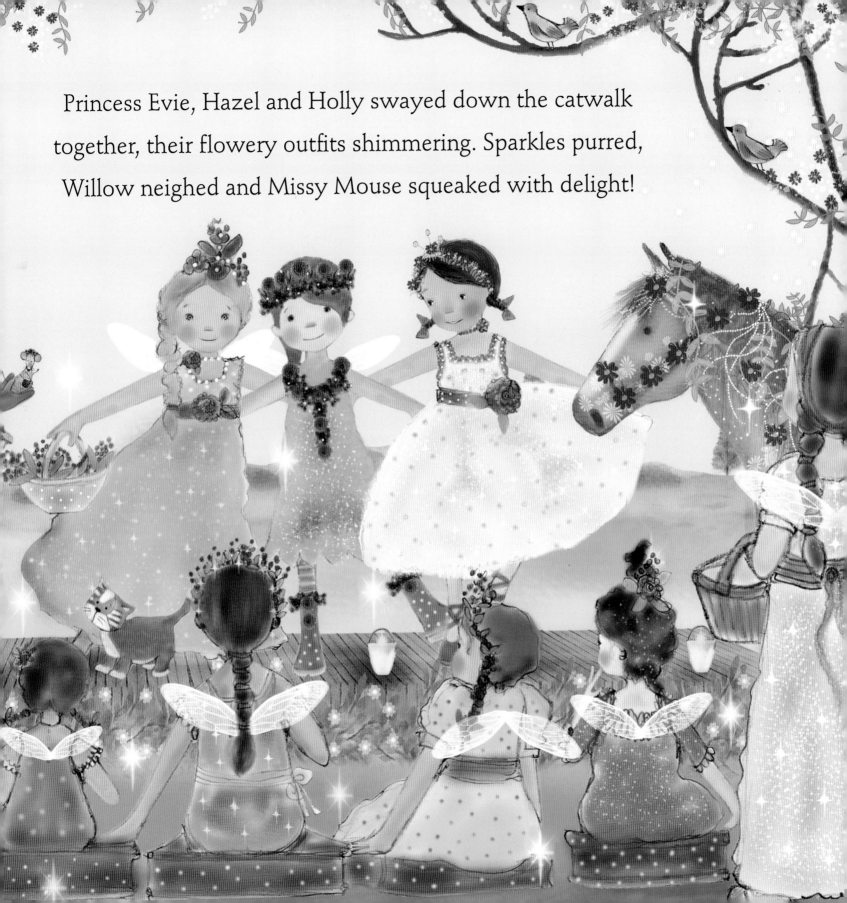

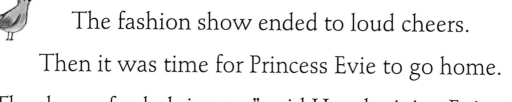

The fashion show ended to loud cheers.

Then it was time for Princess Evie to go home.

"Thank you for helping us," said Hazel, giving Evie a hug.

"You helped the Bluebell Forest Fashion Show happen!"

said Holly. "We'll never forget you."

Princess Evie and Sparkles hopped onto Willow's back and trotted off towards the tunnel of trees. Evie turned to wave at the dancing forest fairies as they grew smaller in the distance.

Back at Starlight Stables, Princess Evie led
Willow to her stall and there, pinned onto
the door, was a golden invitation.

"It's from the forest fairies," gasped Princess Evie. "They want us to be guests of honour at their next fashion show! Oh, thank you, fairies!"

Evie brushed out Willow's shining coat and mane.
"And thank you, Willow, for taking me to Bluebell Forest,"
she smiled. "You're a VERY special forest pony!"
"Miaow," agreed Sparkles.

Also available:

Neptune the Magic Sea Pony

Shimmer the Magic Ice Pony

Silver the Magic Snow Pony

Star the Magic Sand Pony

Coming soon:

Indigo the Magic
Rainbow Pony